Have a great summer.
See you next year around McKinley.
-Blaine

Too bad we didn't hang out more...
Sam

I think you are totally UNICORN!
cu next year!
Brittany

It's BEEN REAL.

U R Artie
2 good
2 B
forgotten
Tina

Keep on dancing.
-Mike

Don't ever forget me!
See you backstage.

Rachel

YOU MAKE ME GO,
"HUBBA, HUBBA!"
-Jacob

You. Me.
Let's bring the sexy back.
Puck

Peace, Love, and HAGS
(Have a great summer)
-Mercedes

Quinn

Love your style.
Will miss you loads.
Kurt

Life's a bitch and then you die. Have a great summer! -Lauren

I'll see you around. See you soon.
S- It's all inside of you to be successful!
You can do it!
-Will Schuester

WHAT ARE YOU SUPPOSED TO WRITE ON THESE THINGS?
Umm...GO TITANS!
FINN

McKINLEY ★ THUNDERCLAP ★

M

Poppy

Hachette Book Group
237 Park Avenue, New York, NY 10017
For more of your favorite series and novels,
go to www.pickapoppy.com

Poppy is an imprint of Little, Brown and Company.
The Poppy name and logo are trademarks of Hachette Book Group, Inc.

The publisher is not responsible for websites (or their content) that are not owned by the publisher.

First Edition: May 2012

ISBN 978-0-316-12358-7

10 9 8 7 6 5 4 3 2 1

WOR

Interior book design: Georgia Rucker Design
Show graphic design by Jason Sweers

Stock art: pp. 6-7: L.Watcharapol/shutterstock.com; p. 10 and throughout: (film frame) hellena13/shutterstock.com; p. 10: (star charm) BW Folsom/shutterstock.com; pp. 10-13: (stars) Smileus/shutterstock.com; p. 18: (notebook) MilousSK/shutterstock.com; pp. 18, 20 (stars) Smileus/shutterstock.com; pp. 38-41: (lipstick kiss) vlad_star/shutterstock.com; pp. 44-45: (background doodles) blue67design/shutterstock.com; pp. 46-47: (pencils) Julia Ivantsova/shutterstock.com; pp. 54-55: (notebook) tovovan/shutterstock.com; pp. 56-61: (photography illustrations) pixbox77/shutterstock.com; pp. 76-77: (green background) Picsfive/shutterstock.com; p. 78: (sombreros) Basheera Designs/shutterstock.com; pp. 78-85: (rulers) ruslanchik/shutterstock.com; p. 86: (lunch bag) Fotoline/shutterstock.com; p. 92: (notebook) Mazzzur/shutterstock.com; pp. 92-93, 96: (tape) Picsfive/shutterstock.com; pp. 96-97: (paper) vovan/shutterstock.com; p. 98: (white paper) helissente/shutterstock.com, (pink notes) George Pappas/shutterstock.com, (lined note) Brian Weed/shutterstock.com; p. 99: (lined notes, top and bottom right) Gregory Dunn/shutterstock.com, (three unlined notes) hfng/shutterstock.com, (bottom lined note) 89studio/shutterstock.com; p. 136: (gold frames) Margo Harrison/shutterstock.com; p. 139 (piano illustration) Brailescu Cristian/shutterstock.com.

Printed in the United States of America

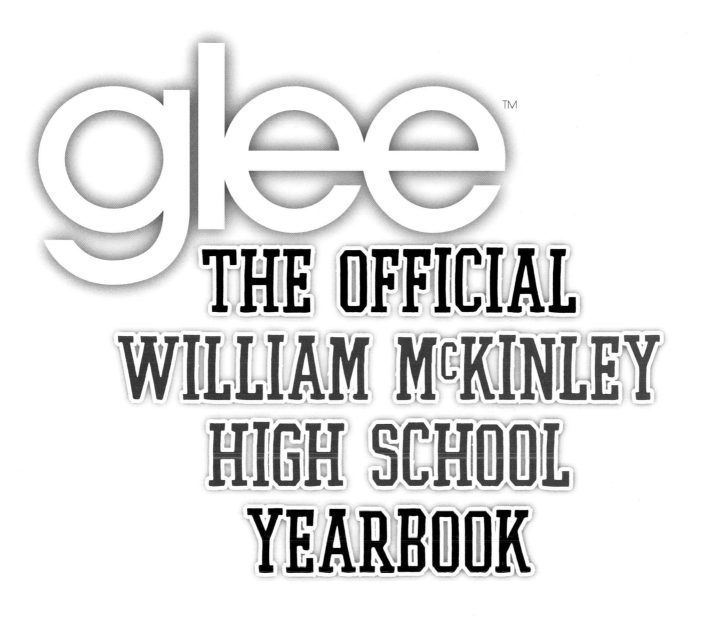

glee™

THE OFFICIAL WILLIAM McKINLEY HIGH SCHOOL YEARBOOK

YEARBOOK EDITOR:

Debra Mostow Zakarin

poppy

Little, Brown and Company
New York ★ Boston

AND HERE'S WHAT YOU NEED TO KNOW ABOUT McKINLEY HIGH...

MASCOT: Titans

COLORS: red and white

NAMED AFTER: the 25th president of the United States, William McKinley Jr.

LOCATION: Lima, Ohio

FAMOUS PEOPLE TO MATRICULATE FROM McKINLEY HIGH SCHOOL:

Rachel Berry

FROM THE DESK OF FIGGINS

WMHS

Dear McKinley High students,

What a year this has been! There was a leprechaun roaming the halls, we endured something called "Booty Camp," and we averted the toilet-paper shortage crisis (wipe away, everyone). And, of course, we learned a great deal about competition!

We witnessed a heated congressional race, a student body election, and the battle between New Directions and the Warblers. It is of importance to note that this year we are pleased Glee Club is included in the yearbook. All in all, this has been a year where we didn't go over budget and we made it through without too many incidents. (Again, our sincerest apologies to the students who ate the ravioli and needed to get tetanus shots.)

As you venture out into the world, don't forget that you are forever a Titan. Be proud to say you came from McKinley High.

Yours truly,

Principal Figgins

Students

HS!

RACHEL BERRY

I'LL ALWAYS BELIEVE IN: ME (AND BARBRA)

PASSIONS: singing solos, Broadway, Finn, New York City

CLUB: Glee Club

INSPIRATIONS: Barbra Streisand and Patti LuPone

FAVORITE SLUSHIE FLAVOR: grape

> "Metaphors are important. My gold stars are a metaphor, for me, being a star."

"Aside from nudity and the exploitation of animals, I'll pretty much do anything to break into the business."

"Whether it's a heart attack or heartbreak, just like Broadway, the show must go on."

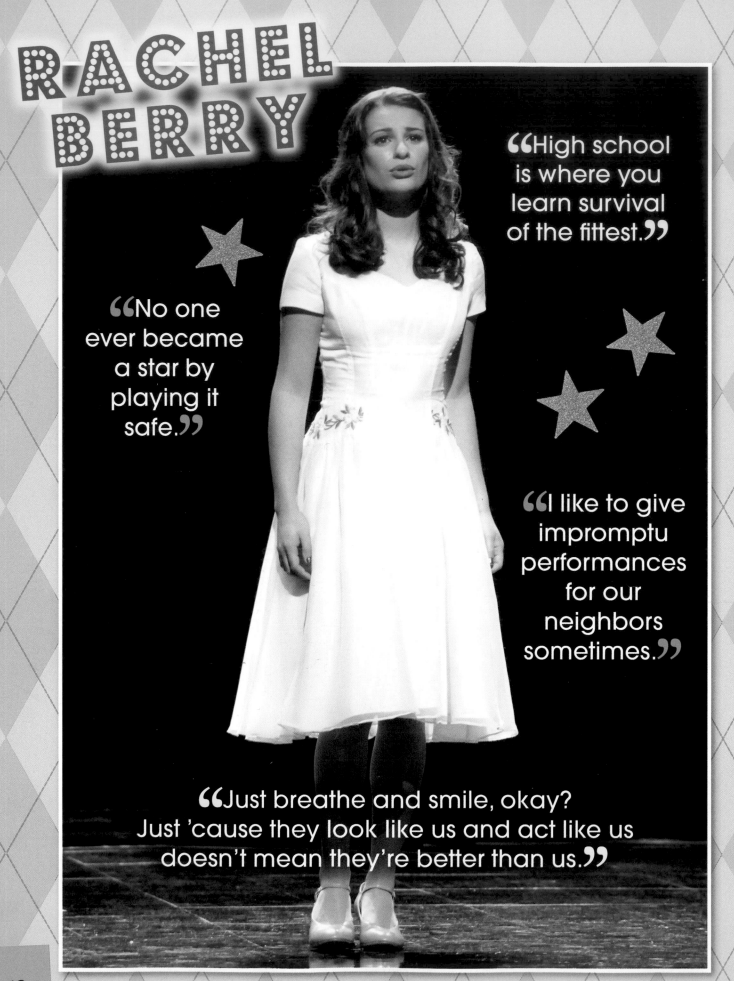

RACHEL BERRY

"High school is where you learn survival of the fittest."

"No one ever became a star by playing it safe."

"I like to give impromptu performances for our neighbors sometimes."

"Just breathe and smile, okay? Just 'cause they look like us and act like us doesn't mean they're better than us."

"There is nothing ironic about show choir!"

"I need applause to live."

"I would rather be a star than be liked."

FINN HUDSON

I'LL ALWAYS
BELIEVE IN:
DOING WHAT
I LOVE

PASSIONS: girls, singing, football

TEAM NUMBER: 5

MOTTO: "If you forget the words, just keep your lips moving. Hopefully, nobody will notice."

"I sort of worship Eric Clapton and Ochocinco."

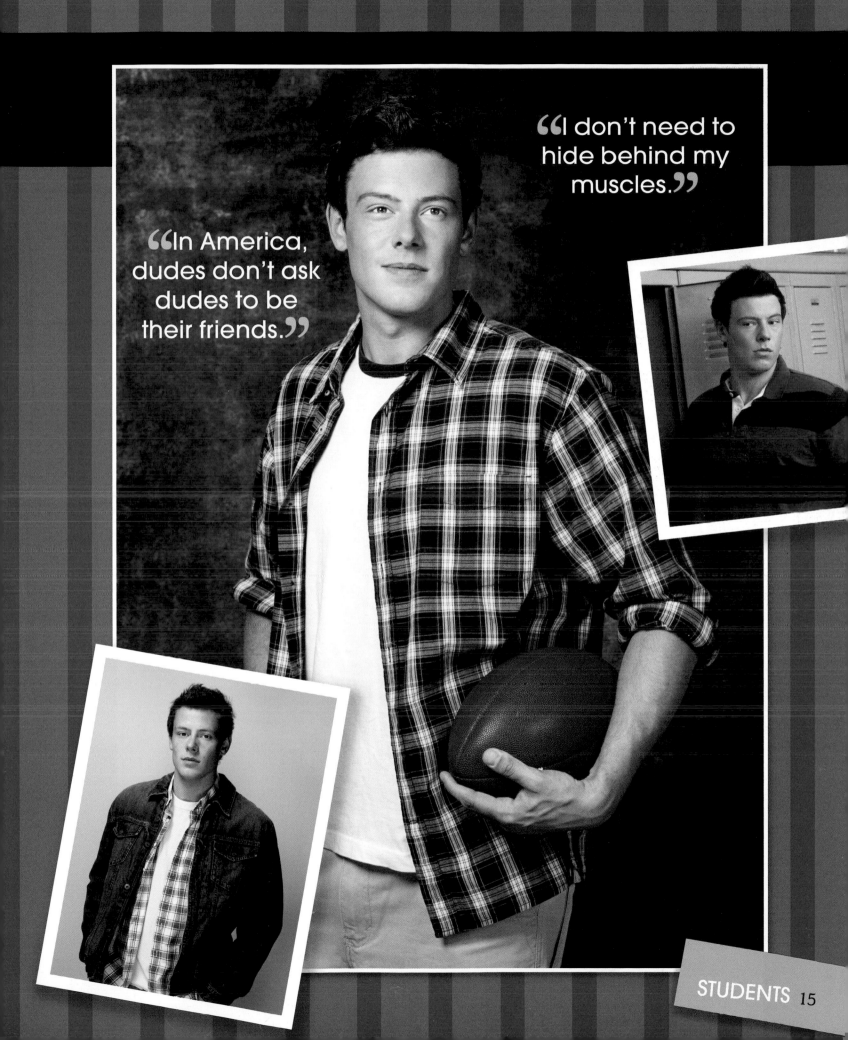

"In America, dudes don't ask dudes to be their friends."

"I don't need to hide behind my muscles."

FINN HUDSON

"Glee's about learning how to accept yourself for who you are, no matter what other people think. And that's what this music is all about."

"My dancing kind of bothers me. Uh, it almost killed Rachel, but I like the way I look."

kurt hummel

I'LL ALWAYS BELIEVE IN:
EXPRESSING MYSELF

PASSIONS: musical theater, fashion, Blaine, makeovers

CLUBS: Glee Club, football

INSPIRATION: Patti LuPone

MOTTO: "When you're different, when you're special, sometimes you have to get used to being alone."

COURAGE

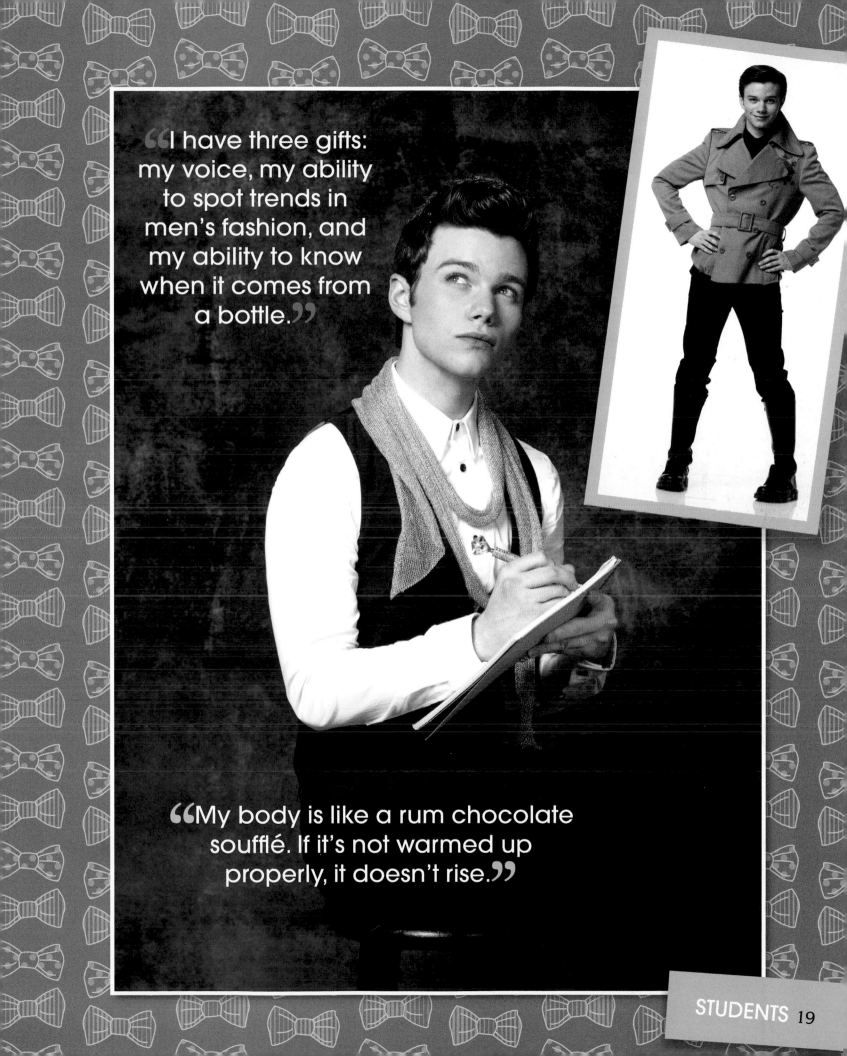

"I have three gifts: my voice, my ability to spot trends in men's fashion, and my ability to know when it comes from a bottle."

"My body is like a rum chocolate soufflé. If it's not warmed up properly, it doesn't rise."

kurt hummel

"We have all felt the cold humiliation of a slushie in the face."

"I don't believe in denying who you are, but I don't believe in outing, either.

"Real brave with your fists, but you're a coward when it comes to the truth.

"Rachel and I might as well get used to a life of barista work and summer stock."

"Everyone knows I'm here doing one thing: dance!"

Mike Chang

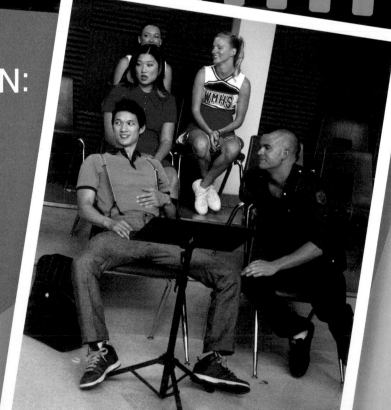

I'LL ALWAYS BELIEVE IN: POP AND LOCK

PASSIONS: dancing, showing off abs, Tina

CLUBS: Glee Club, football, Brainiacs

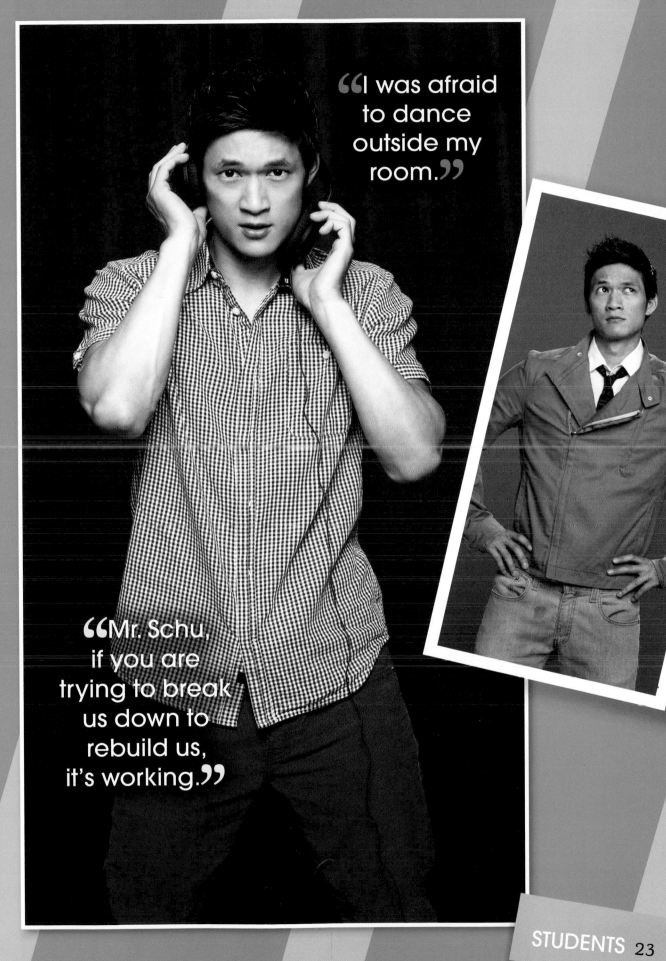

"I was afraid to dance outside my room."

"Mr. Schu, if you are trying to break us down to rebuild us, it's working."

Mike Chang

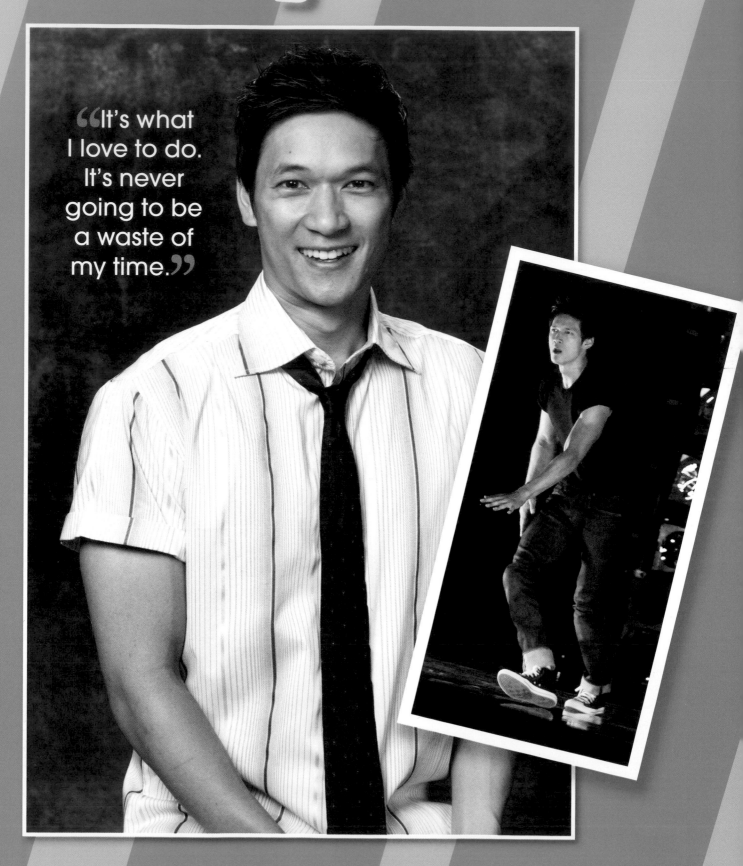

"It's what I love to do. It's never going to be a waste of my time."

"I told my mom I had the flu, and she made me a traditional tea made out of panda hair."

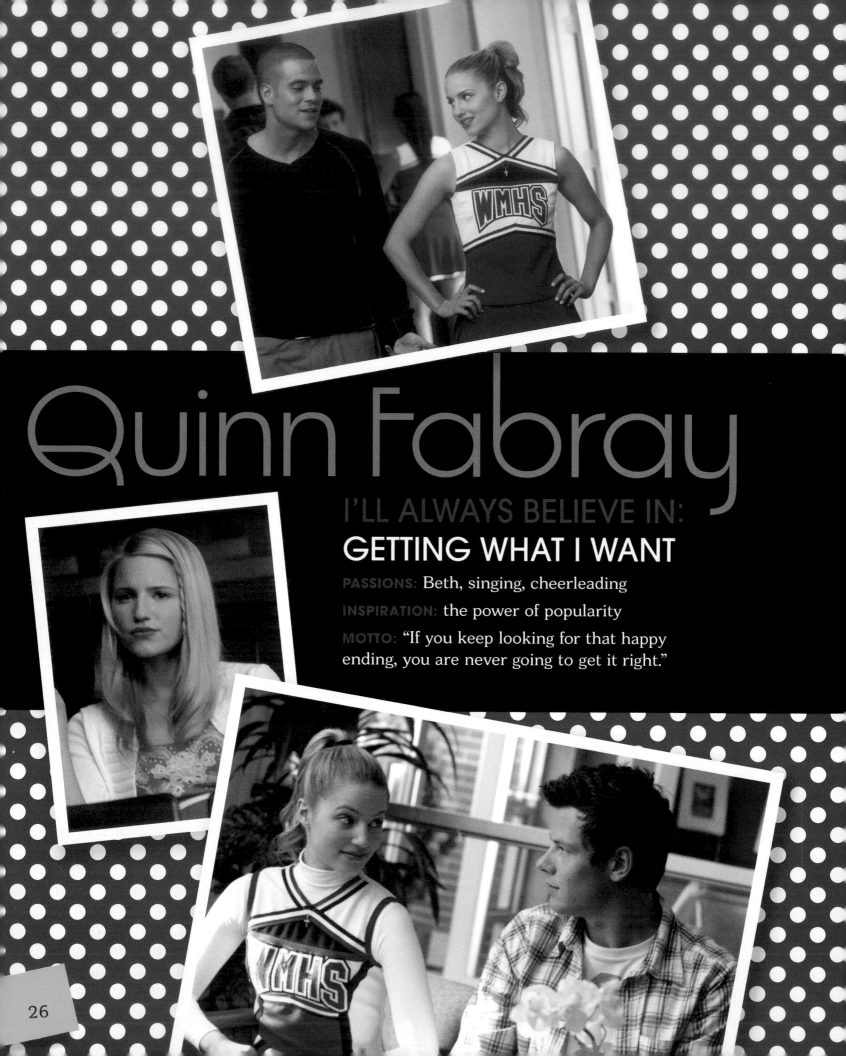

Quinn Fabray

I'LL ALWAYS BELIEVE IN:
GETTING WHAT I WANT

PASSIONS: Beth, singing, cheerleading

INSPIRATION: the power of popularity

MOTTO: "If you keep looking for that happy ending, you are never going to get it right."

"I just want somebody to love me."

"Sometimes people have to deal with a little adversity. I learned that at Glee Club."

"I've always been really handy with a nail file."

Quinn Fabray

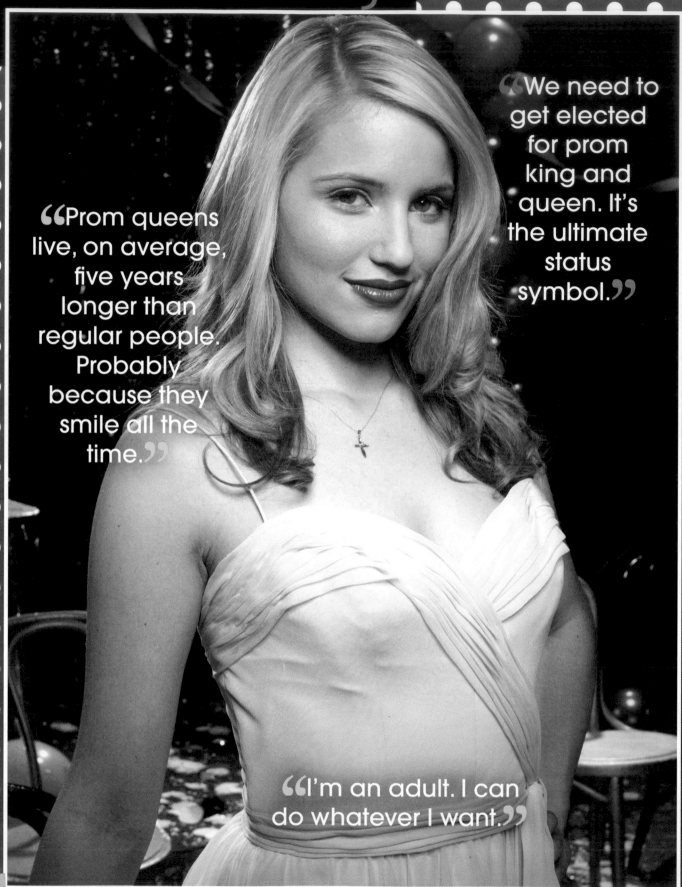

"Prom queens live, on average, five years longer than regular people. Probably because they smile all the time."

"We need to get elected for prom king and queen. It's the ultimate status symbol."

"I'm an adult. I can do whatever I want."

"I've cheated twice in my life. The first time, I got pregnant. The second time, I got mono. I think the universe is trying to tell me something."

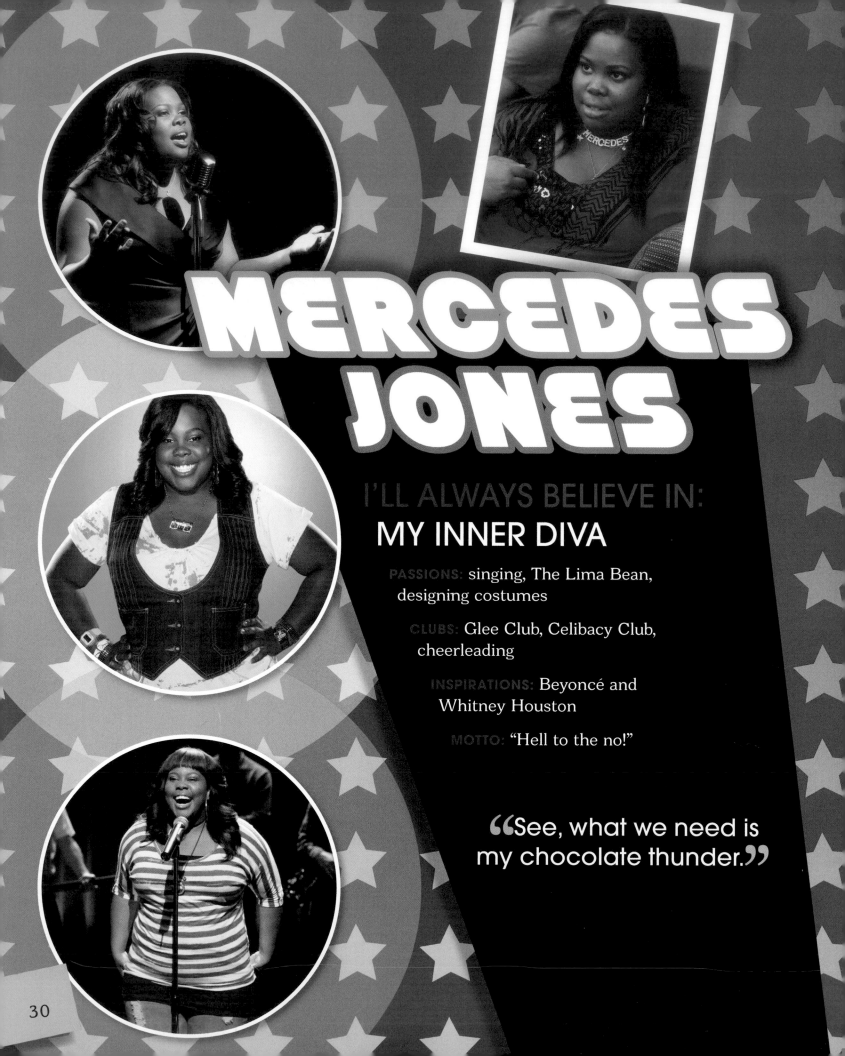

MERCEDES JONES

I'LL ALWAYS BELIEVE IN:
MY INNER DIVA

PASSIONS: singing, The Lima Bean, designing costumes

CLUBS: Glee Club, Celibacy Club, cheerleading

INSPIRATIONS: Beyoncé and Whitney Houston

MOTTO: "Hell to the no!"

"See, what we need is my chocolate thunder."

"Soon as I get my record deal, I'm not speaking to any of you."

"They said JLo's booty was too big."

MERCEDES JONES

"Don't dream it, be it."

"Do you know how hard it is to find high-top, yellow patent leather sneakers?"

NOAH PUCKERMAN

I'LL ALWAYS BELIEVE IN:
COUGARS

PASSIONS: hot older women, hotness of any kind

CLUBS: Glee Club, football, Acafellas

"The thing about chicks is you only have to be a fraction as nice to them as you are mean to them to get them to like you again."

"Hey, losers, tell your mom to call—I'll clean the pool and any other clogged plumbing."

"Turns out Napoleon, not just a dessert—he was a real dude."

NOAH PUCKERMAN

"As far as badasses go, I'm number one."

"She's the one that got away—really, really slowly."

"Dude, my permanent record has three volumes."

"There's no way I'm going back to juvie. There are no chicks and no kosher meal options up in that place."

"I know hickeys. I'm a freakin' connoisseur. I can make them into shapes, like balloon animals."

SANTANA LOPEZ

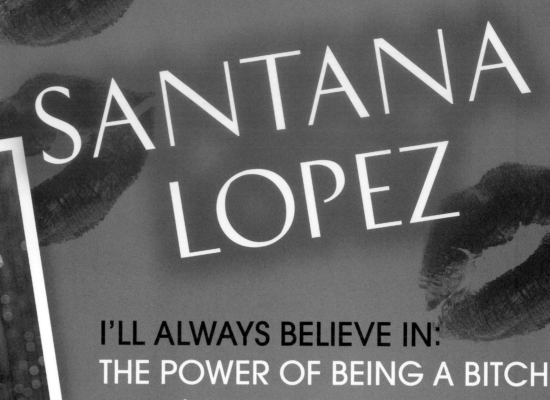

I'LL ALWAYS BELIEVE IN:
THE POWER OF BEING A BITCH

PASSIONS: dancing, singing, Brittany

CLUBS: cheerleading, Glee Club, Bully Whips

MOTTO: "Everyone knows that my job here is to look hot."

"I love girls the way that I'm supposed to feel about boys."

"Just because I hate everybody doesn't mean they have to hate me, too."

"I'm from Lima Heights Adjacent, and I'm proud. Do you know what goes down in Lima Heights Adjacent? Bad things!"

SANTANA LOPEZ

"I know what cheating looks like. I do it all the time."

"I'm keepin' it real."

"Legend has it that when I came out of my mother, I told the nurse she was fat."

Blaine Anderson

I'LL ALWAYS BELIEVE IN: ROMANCE

PASSIONS: singing, acting, Roxy Music, football, Kurt

CLUB: Glee Club

INSPIRATIONS: Katy Perry, Marion Cotillard

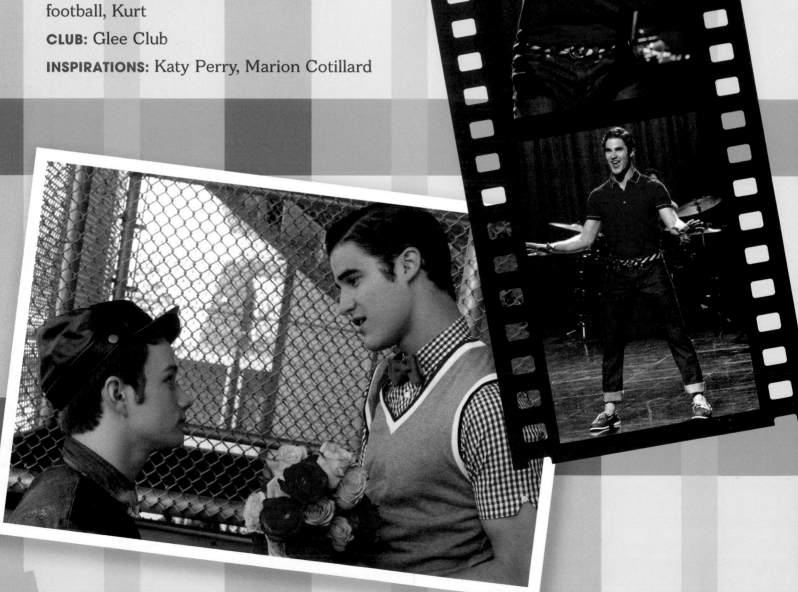

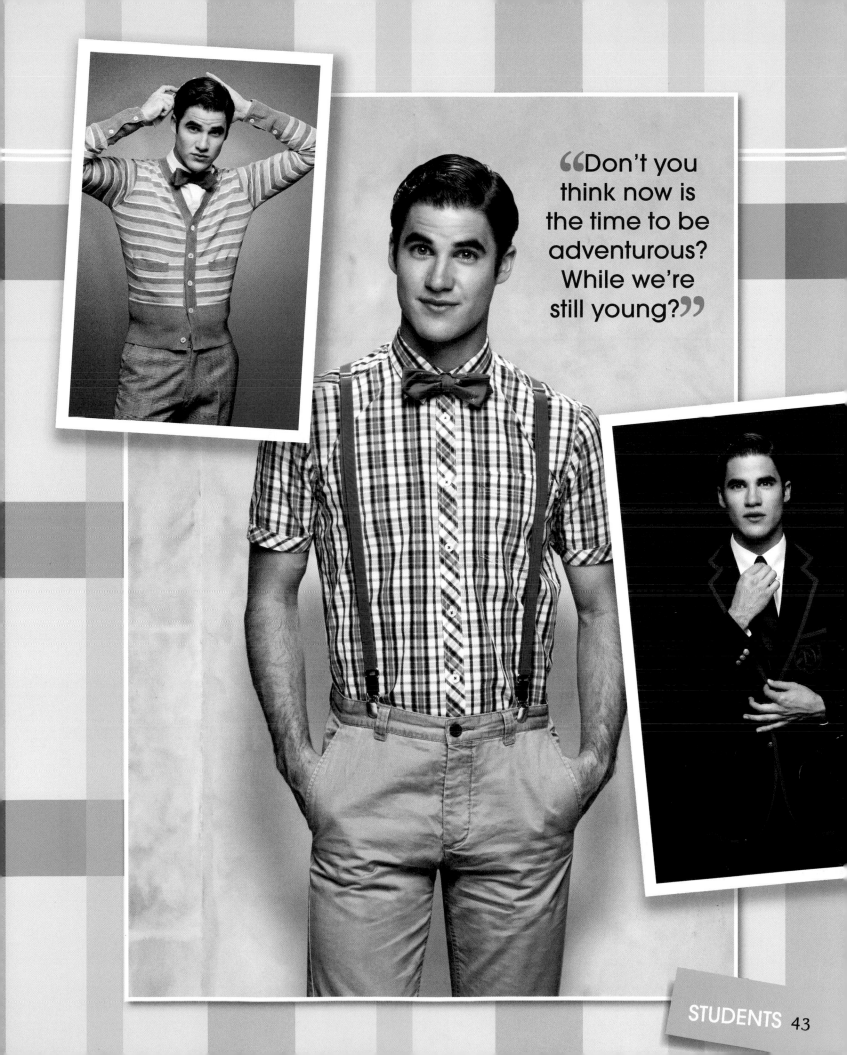

❝Don't you think now is the time to be adventurous? While we're still young?❞

Brittany S. Pierce

I'LL ALWAYS BELIEVE IN: MAGIC

PASSIONS: hosting *Fondue for Two*, Santana, dancing, singing, trendsetting

CLUBS: cheerleading, Glee Club, Brainiacs

INSPIRATIONS: unicorns, Santa Claus, cats

"Did you know that dolphins are just gay sharks?"

"Most teachers think that by cutting class, I might improve my grades."

"Everybody, drink responsibly."

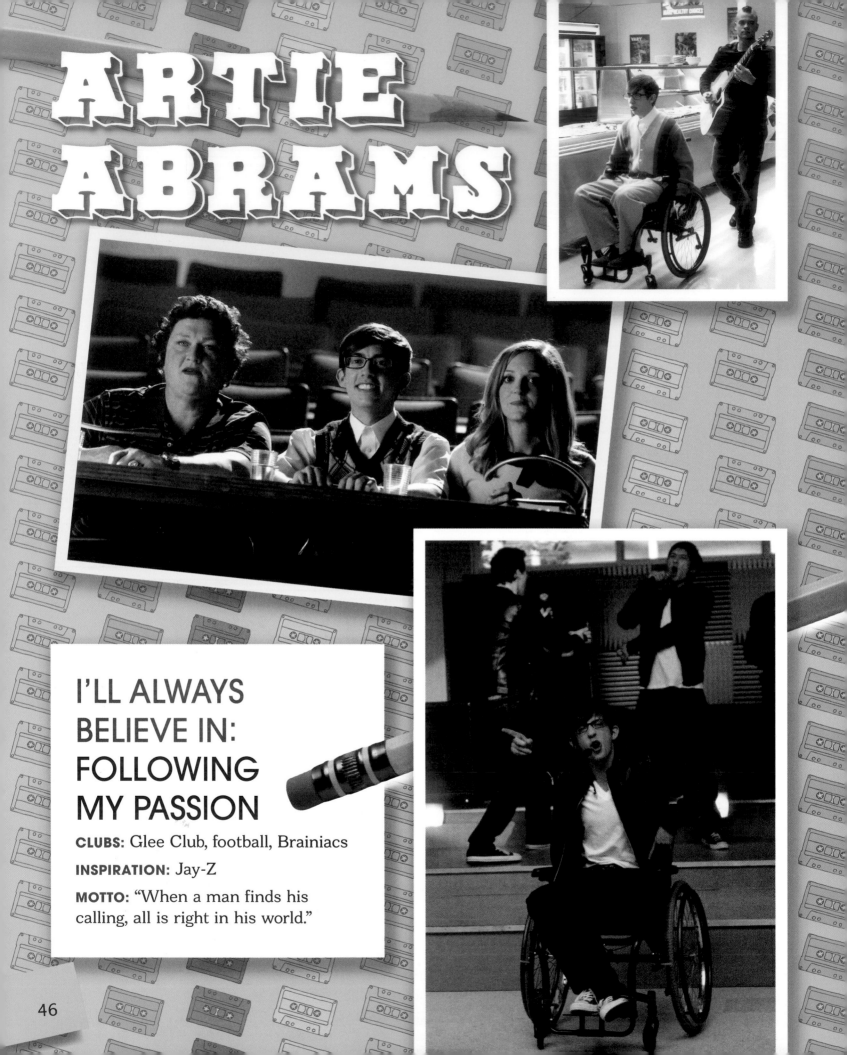

ARTIE ABRAMS

I'LL ALWAYS BELIEVE IN: FOLLOWING MY PASSION

CLUBS: Glee Club, football, Brainiacs

INSPIRATION: Jay-Z

MOTTO: "When a man finds his calling, all is right in his world."

"I'm never gonna dunk a basketball or kill a lion. I need to focus on dreams I can make come true."

"I'm just a stud in a chair."

Tina Cohen-Chang

I'LL ALWAYS BELIEVE IN: BEING MYSELF

PASSIONS: singing, dancing, Mike, Mike's abs

CLUBS: Glee Club, football, Brainiacs

INSPIRATION: Asian vampires

MOTTO: "I'm in love with myself, and I would never change a thing."

"I'm so overcome with love! I love you, Mike Chang!"

"If I have
no Asian sex
symbols to
look up to,
I guess I'll just
have to be
one myself."

"If you can
imagine it,
it can come
true."

STUDENT LIFE

"Everything Bieber does is epic." —SAM EVANS

"If I was a country, my flag would be a big fist giving the rest of the world the finger." —LAUREN ZIZES

"Technology has allowed us to be brutally cruel without suffering any consequences. In the past, if I wanted to tell someone they sucked, I'd have to say it to their face." —JACOB BEN ISRAEL

"When I saw you guys singing and dancing in the cafeteria, I thought, 'I am so much better than you.'" —SUGAR MOTTA

THE HALLWAYS

"You think before I cleat some dude I hug him?" —SHANE TINSLEY

"I love everything about America, especially NASCAR, your half-black president, and Victoria's Secret catalogs." —RORY FLANAGAN

"This is high school. People's memories for good stuff last about as long as their Facebook status." —DAVE KAROFSKY

"Coach, no disrespect, but my dad, he didn't raise me to be no damn ballerina. In fact, my dad, he didn't even raise me." —AZIMIO ADAMS

McKinley High Student Most Likely to...

Design his own brand of jeans (or become an event planner):
Kurt

Be pulled over driving a Segway® on the highway (or become a time-travel tour guide):
Brittany

Perform at a Super Bowl halftime:
Mercedes

Be the head of the McKinley High Glee Club in ten years:
Finn

Become mayor
of Lima Heights:
Santana

Star in his own reality show:
Puck

Have a New Directions-
themed wedding:
Mike and Tina

Run a recording studio:
Artie

Host the Tony Awards:
Rachel

Perform on cruise ships:
Sam

Be a househusband:
Blaine

That song was so depressing. I may actually be dead now.

Being a hot seventeen-year-old, you can get away with or do anything you want.

Kurtcedes

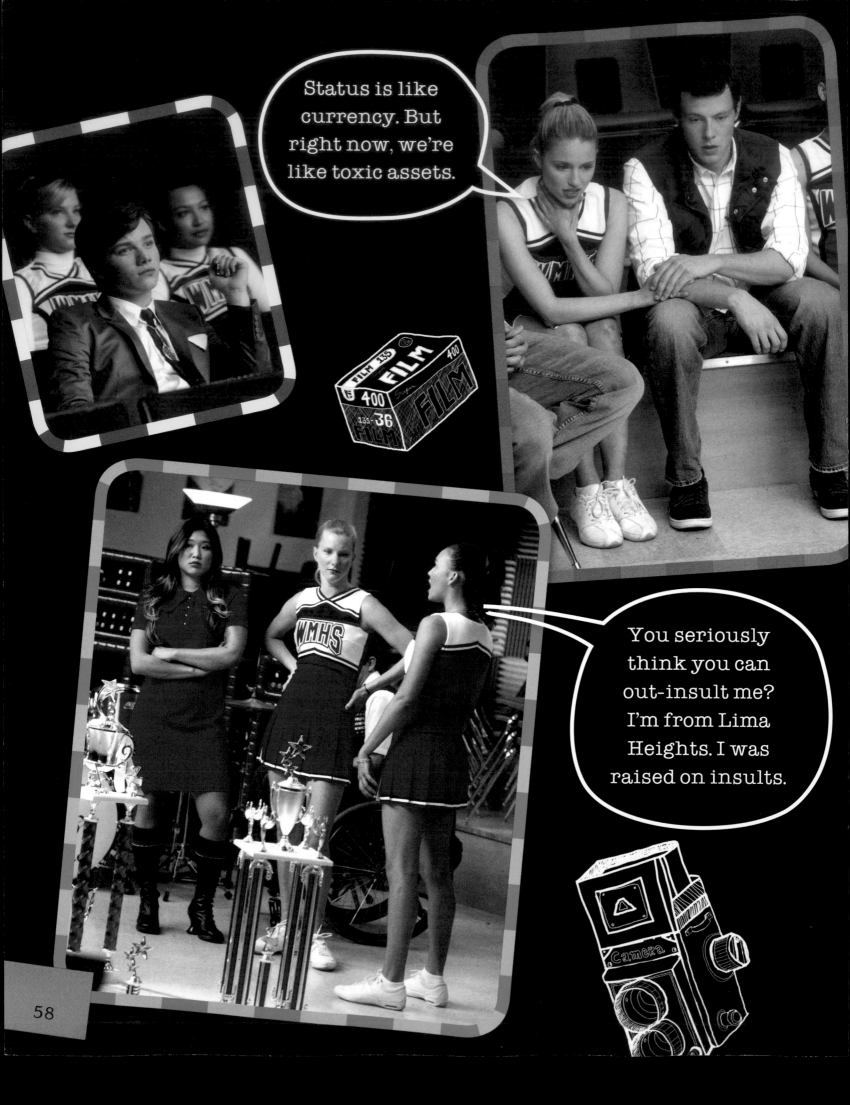

When I see you dance, that's why I fell in love with you.

A unicorn is someone who knows he's popular but isn't afraid to show it.

I want my senior year to be magic. And that's only gonna happen if I spend every minute of every day with you.

At this school, the thing that makes you different is the thing that people use to crush your spirit.

A little something-something always leads to something more. I've been there. Remember?

SLUSHIE FACIALS

The Big Quench: Terrorizing Titans Since 1992!

REMEMBER WHEN...

Santana made a voodoo doll of Rachel.

Finn believed in the Grilled Cheesus.

Sue Sylvester almost stole Christmas.

Brittany believed in a magic comb.

Puck was in juvie.

Rachel duct-taped her mouth.

Santana purposely gave Finn and Quinn mono.

Finn accidentally broke Rachel's nose.

Emma Pillsbury almost married Ken Tanaka.

Sue Sylvester was principal.

Quinn was a skank.

Puck liked Lauren.

REMEMBER WHEN....

Rachel had a crush on Will Schuester.

Finn and Quinn were in love.

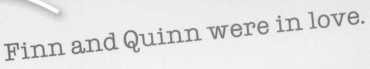

Kurt was on the football team.

"Hi, I'm Kurt Hummel, and I'll be auditioning for the role of kicker."

Will Schuester formed the Acafellas.

The football team channeled Michael Jackson at halftime.

Rachel was Jesse St. James's girlfriend.

Santana and Karofsky "dated."

New Directions was cast in a mattress commerical.

REMEMBER WHEN...?

The football team danced to Beyoncé.

Santana got a boob job.

Sue married herself.

Brittany competed at the academic decathlon competition.

Rachel stuffed the ballot boxes.
"Who can blame a gal desperate not to move to NYC without her best gay? What if she required an emergency makeover or a soufflé?"

Mercedes and Rachel had a "diva-off."

Finn and Rachel's kiss made New Directions lose at Nationals.

Rachel was going to wait until she was twenty-five years old to lose her virginity.

REMEMBER WHEN...

Rachel, Mercedes, and Sam had a three-way, as one another's dates to prom.

Rachel wanted Quinn's nose.

"It's less Hebraic and more Fabray-ic"

kurt

Finn and Rachel went on a stakeout.

Kurt was prom queen.
"Eat your heart out, Kate Middleton."

Kurt was a Warbler.

Karofsky was a bully and then a Bully Whip.

A-

Mike got an A- (aka an Asian F).

Artie was Puck's community service.

Artie joined the football team.

The football team locked Puck in a portable toilet.

Tina and Santana wrote "Trouty Mouth."

SPIRIT DAYS

WE'RE #1 WMHS

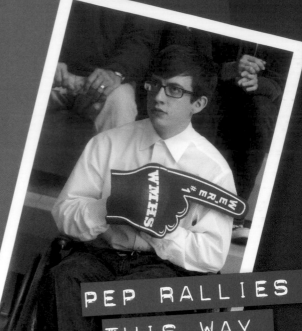

PEP RALLIES THIS WAY.

WMHS

MERCEDES AND KURT TAKE CENTER COURT AT A PEP RALLY.

MCKINLEY TEAM BOOSTER

FOR A GOOD CAUSE

THE KISSER IS OUT

WMHS GLEE CLUB Handicapable BUS BAKE SALE

FLIRTING AT THE BAKE SALE

WMHS

GLEE CLUB SOLD TITAN RED CUPCAKES TO RAISE $600 FOR ARTIE'S BUS.

BAKE SALE

3/2012

Will Schuester

**SPANISH TEACHER,
GLEE CLUB DIRECTOR,
EX-DETENTION DIRECTOR**

FAVORITE SONG: any power ballad
SOFT SPOT: eighties music
MOTTO: "Life really has only one beginning and one end. The rest is just a whole lot of middle."

"Glee Club... it's about expressing yourself to yourself."

"Everybody LOVES disco!"

Sue Sylvester

**CHEERLEADING COACH,
AURAL INTENSITY COACH,
FORMER GLEE CLUB DIRECTOR**

CLAIM TO FAME: Top-700 recording artist

POSITIVE QUALITIES: vindictive, spiteful, pompous, vain

GOAL: to turn the United States into a monarchy

FAVORITE SONG: anything that's not a power ballad

INSPIRATION: Madonna

NOTE FROM COACH SYLVESTER: "All other inquiries, media-related or not, should be referred to my legal counsel."

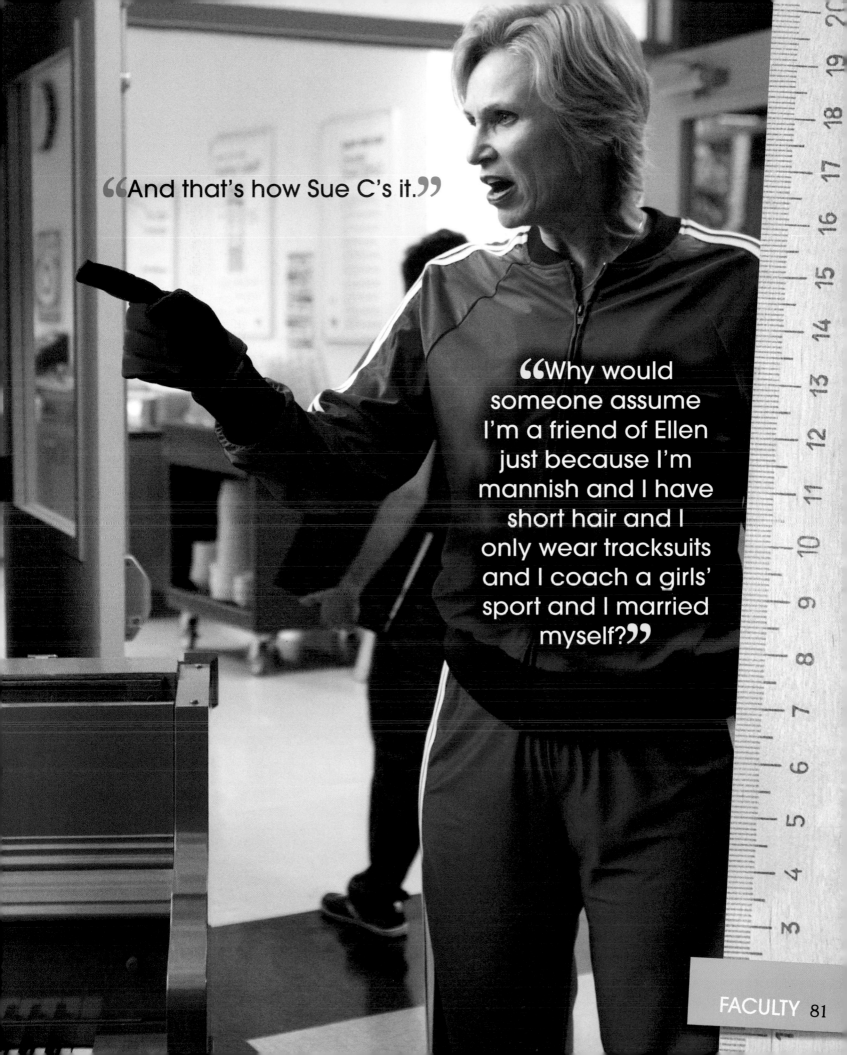

"And that's how Sue C's it."

"Why would someone assume I'm a friend of Ellen just because I'm mannish and I have short hair and I only wear tracksuits and I coach a girls' sport and I married myself?"

Shannon Beiste

FOOTBALL COACH

HOBBY: line dancing

MOTTO: "I run the S.S. *Kick-Ass*, not the S.S. *Backtalk*."

FAVORITE SONG: anything country

"You ain't lived till you've seen me in a... cowboy hat!"

"I'm such a girl."

Emma Pillsbury

**GUIDANCE COUNSELOR,
FACULTY ADVISER FOR THE CELIBACY CLUB**

INSPIRATION: Julie Andrews
CHILDHOOD DREAM: to be a dairy farmer

DRUGS ARE LAME.

LIMA PUBLIC SCHOOLS DRUG PREVENTION

AIDS

SYPHILIS

GONORRHEA

CHLAMYDIA

LICE

HERPES

VAGINITIS

GENITAL WARTS

CRABS

STD's
SEXUALLY TRANSMITTED DISEASES
DON'T PASS THEM ON!

"At what age are you allowed to look back on your life with nothing but regret?"

"It always freaks me out to eat candy that someone else has touched."

88

Sue vs. Schu

Will: Let's bury the hatchet, Sue.

Sue: No, I won't be burying any hatchet. Unless I get a clear shot to your groin!

- -

Will: Inside, you're a really good person. I appreciate what you're doing for these kids. I won't forget it.

Sue: I'm seriously gonna puke in your mouth.

- -

Will: I love my kids.

Sue: You do with your depressing little group of kids what I did with my wealthy, elderly mother: Euthanize it. It's time.

Will: Not the point of Glee Club, Sue.

- -

Sue: Where's the hate?

Will: You know what you are, Sue? You're a Grinch.

- -

Sue: I don't trust a man with curly hair. I can't help but picture little birds laying sulfurous eggs in there, and it disgusts me.

- -

Will: Your pom-pom budget is $4,000 a month!

Sue: You can't put a price on cheer.

- -

Will: I thought you hated the holidays.

Sue: No, I just hate you!

- -

Will: You have always been out to get me.

Sue: If I were out to get you, you'd be pickling in a mason jar on my shelf by now.

ROVING REPORTER

Jacob Ben Israel here, the yearbook roving reporter, getting you all the dish you want and need!

P.S. Rachel, if you're reading this, I want to ravage you.

J.B.I. + R.B. 4 ΣVA

WAITING FOR THEIR SOLOS

RUMOR HAS IT

The McKinley High Hookup Map

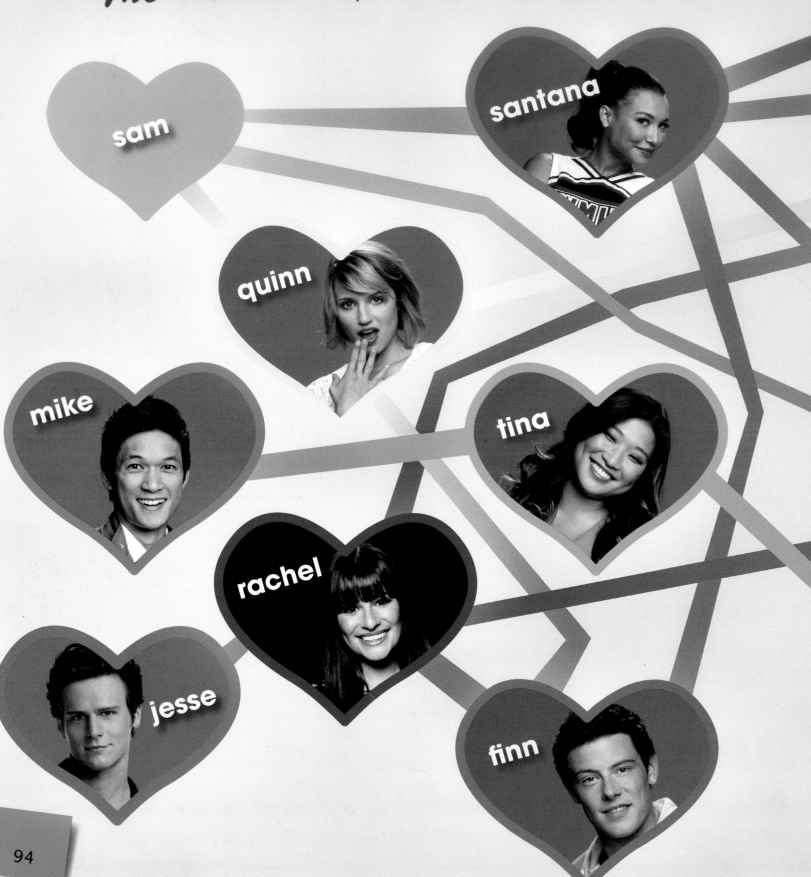

karofsky

puck

blaine

lauren

artie

kurt

brittany

shane

mercedes

Dear Journal,

Feeling listless again today. It began at dawn, when I tried to make a smoothie out of beef bones, breaking my juicer. And then at practice—disaster. It was unmistakable. It was like spotting the first spark on the Hindenburg—a quiver. That quiver will lose us Nationals. And without a championship, I will lose my endorsements. And without those endorsements, I won't be able to buy my hovercraft.

Dear Journal,

Glee-e-e-e Club. Every time I try to destroy that clutch of scab-eating mouth-breathers, it only comes back stronger, like a sexually ambiguous horror movie villain. Here I am, about to turn 30, and I've sacrificed everything only to be shanghaied by the bicurious machinations of a cabal of doughy, misshapen teens.

Am I missing somethi[ng] Journal? Is it me?

Of course its not me. Its Will

trash
or
Treasure?

Notes from the Bin

WHILE YOU WERE OUT

For _Principal Figgins_   Time _____ A.M. P.M.

Date _____

M _Parent_

Of _____

☐ Phone _____

☐ Fax _____

☐ Mobile _____

Area Code   Number   Extension

TELEPHONED		PLEASE CALL	
CAME TO SEE YOU		WILL CALL AGAIN	
WANTS TO SEE YOU		URGENT	
RETURNED YOUR CALL		SPECIAL ATTENTION	

Message _Parent called to find out why the kids are being served prison food for lunch. Call back to discuss immediately._

Meet me at Breadstix— u-know-who is in serious need of a gayvention.

HOW 'BOUT WE NAME THE BABY DRIZZLE?

WHILE YOU WERE OUT

For _Principal Figgins_

Date _____   Time _____ A.M. P.M.

M _Sue_

Of _____

☐ Phone _____

☐ Fax _____

☐ Mobile _____

Area Code

TELEPHONED		Number	
CAME TO SEE YOU			
WANTS TO SEE YOU		PLEASE CALL	Extension
RETURNED YOUR CALL		WILL CALL AGAIN	
Message		URGENT	
		SPECIAL ATTENTION	

Message _Sue called. She says she demands your resignation as principal of this school. And, before you leave, disband Glee Club._

Signed _____

You are totally ~~totally~~ unicorn

I JUST CAUGHT YOU CHECKING OUT MY GUNS.

Finn, check the calendar-updated it.

Finchel, Your mustache needs some combing.

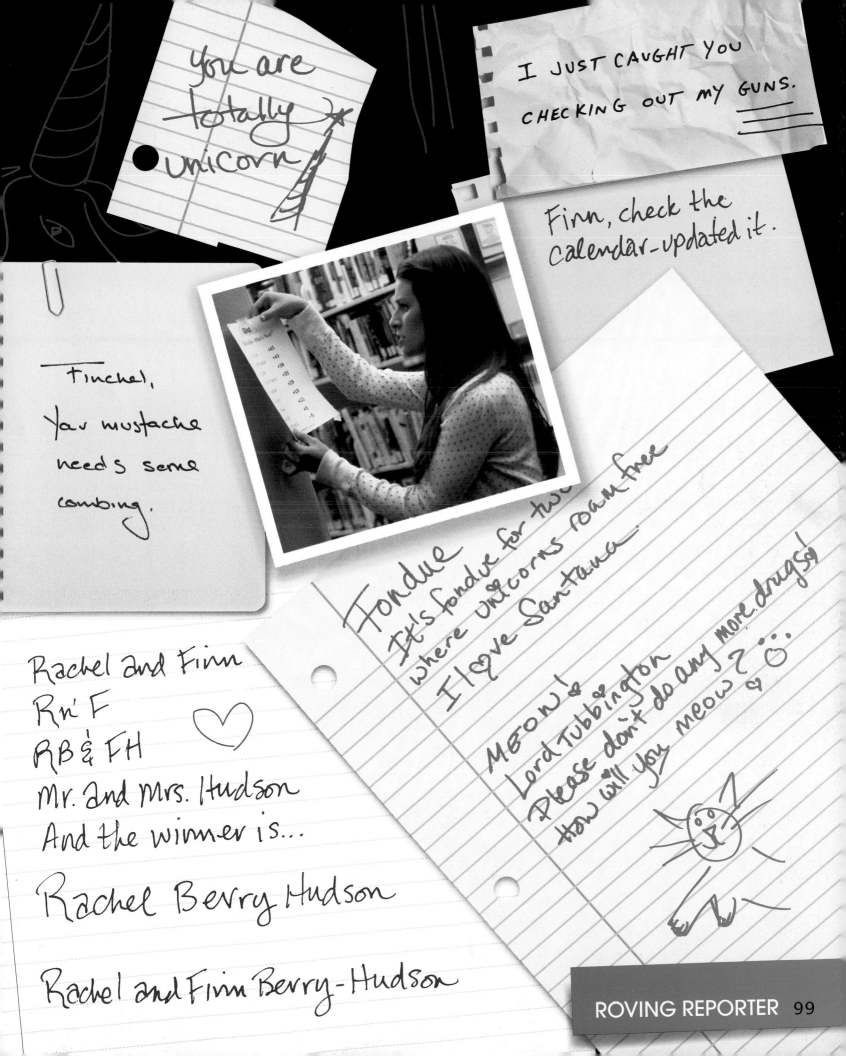

Rachel and Finn
Rn'F
RB & FH ♡
Mr. and Mrs. Hudson
And the winner is...

Rachel Berry Hudson

Rachel and Finn Berry-Hudson

Fondue for two
It's fondue for two
where unicorns roam free
I love Santana

MEOW!
Lord Tubbington
Please don't do any more drugs!
How will you meow ♡

BRITTANY

As a reporter, it's second nature to keep my eyes and ears open at all times. I've seen and heard a lot this year at McKinley. But the best one-liners that I've eavesdropped on have to be from every Titan's favorite ditzy blond cheerleader. Brittany, this page is for you.

Lord Tubbington's allowed to eat cheese because he's on Atkins.

This room looks like the one on that spaceship where I got probed.

God, I'm so sad. Like a sad little panda.

My lips move, but only dust comes out.

You know, we used to be like the Three Musketeers, and now Santana and I are like Almond Joy, and you're like a Jolly Rancher that fell in the ashtray.

I was sure that our Nationals trophy would grow during the summer.

I don't brush my teeth. I rinse my mouth out with soda after I eat.

Well, when a pony does a good deed, he gets a horn, and he becomes a unicorn, and he poops out cotton candy, until he forgets he's magical. And then his horn falls off. And black unicorns, they become zebras.

What, Sour Patch Kids are just Gummi Bears that turned to drugs?

She's a girl. Fooling around with her isn't cheating. It's just friends talking with their tongues super close.

When I pulled my hamstring, I went to a misogynist.

My middle name is Susan, my last name is Pierce. That makes me Brittany S. Pierce. "Brittany Spierce." I've lived my entire life in Britney Spears's shadow.

If elected, I will make sure to have sugary treats available at all times. It helps the concentration.

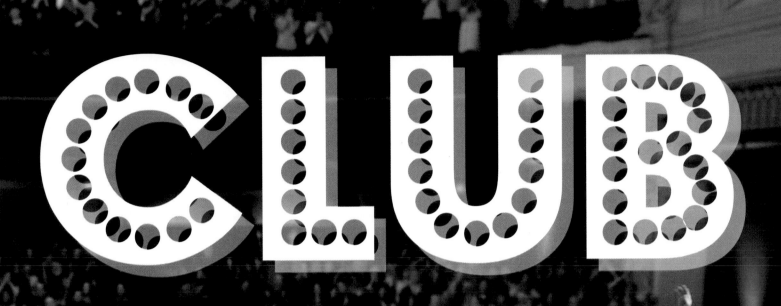

Glee Club is about what's inside you.

New

"Being a part of
something special—
it made me special."
—TINA

Directions

GLEE CLUB FEELING THE RHYTHM OF THE BEAT

"You're just as ambitious as I am; that's why we're friends."

—RACHEL

AUDITIONING FOR "WEST SIDE STORY"

ROLLING TO THE BEAT

"Who cares what happens when we get there when the getting there has been so much fun?"

—WILL

BRINGING THE HOUSE DOWN

CONNECTING WITH HER INNER DIVA

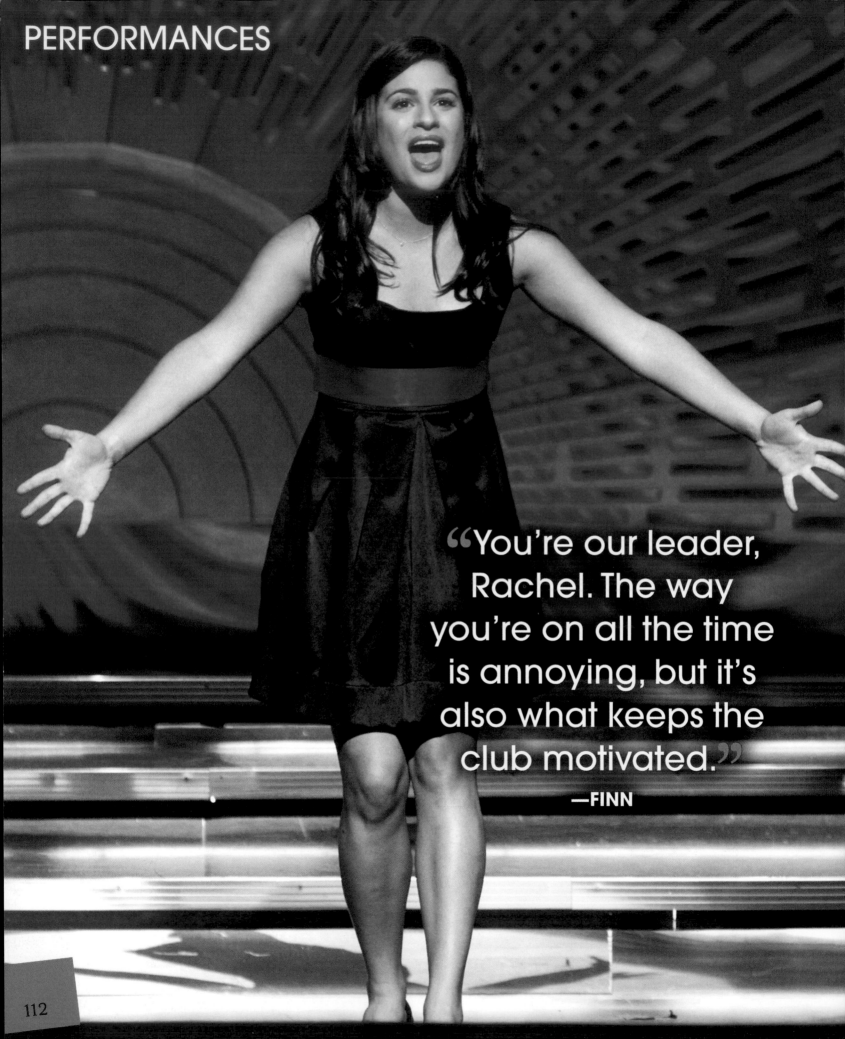

"You're our leader, Rachel. The way you're on all the time is annoying, but it's also what keeps the club motivated."

—FINN

THE POWER OF NEW DIRECTIONS

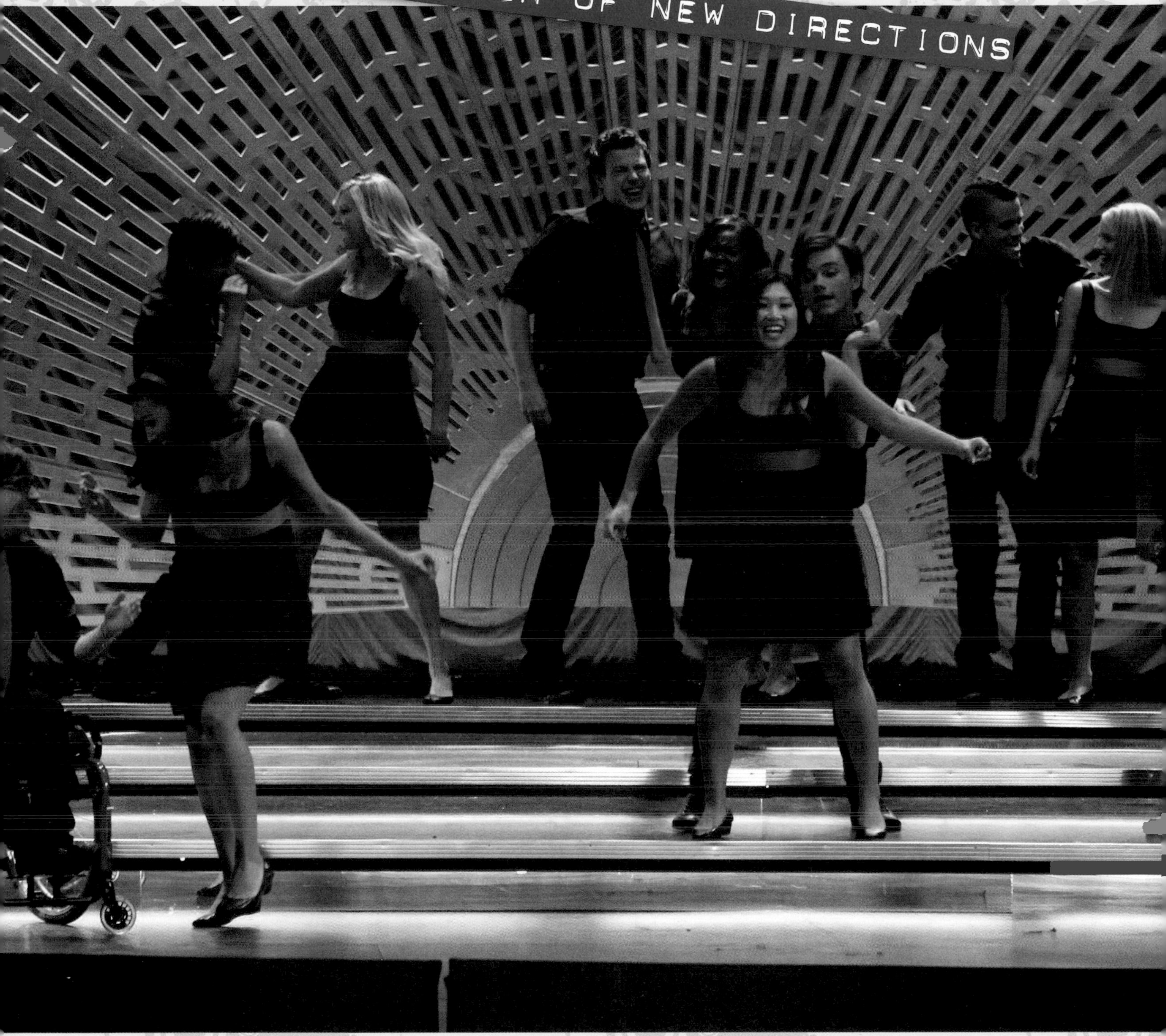

THAT'S SOME SERIOUS ATTITUDE.

"Hairography is all of them whizzing their hair around just to show they're not good dancers."

—RACHEL

SHINING THE LIGHT ON FINN

ENCORE, PLEASE.

"This is the moment in those romantic comedies where I kiss you."

—FINN

NEW YORK, NEW YORK

BROADWAY IS A GIRL'S BEST FRIEND.

ATHL

FOOTBALL

Touching down with the Titans

MCKINLEY FOOTBALL

WHEELING TO
TITAN VICTORY!

CHEER!

I'M SUE SYLVESTER. I HAVE A HUMAN HEART, AND I APPROVE THIS MESSAGE.

Politics is a dirty business and that's why I like it. I thought people wanted a candidate that was for something. That's why I took that pro-deportation stance. But the voters decided to elect a baboon without a heart, and I'm moving on. You know what else is a dirty business? Cheering. Take a look for yourselves. I sponsor this section—by the power of Sue.

SUE'S CORNER
...AND THAT'S HOW SUE C'S IT!

McKINLEY HIGH SCHOOL VARSITY *Cheerleaders*

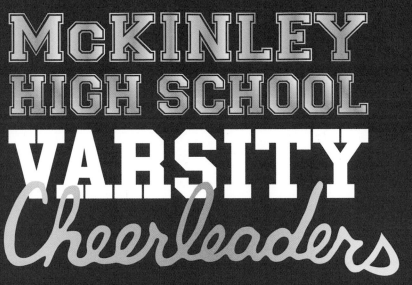

CHEERLEADING: IT *IS* ABOUT WHO WINS.

"First of all, a female football coach, like a male nurse…sin against nature."

"My kids don't love me; they fear me."

"Cheerleading is a sport. There are dangers involved. The same as when a quarterback is sacked, or a hockey player is slammed up against the boards.**"**

"Children must know fear. Without it, they won't know how to behave. They'll try frenching grizzly bears or consider living in Florida.**"**

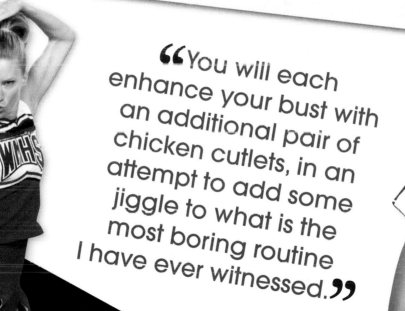

"You will each enhance your bust with an additional pair of chicken cutlets, in an attempt to add some jiggle to what is the most boring routine I have ever witnessed.**"**

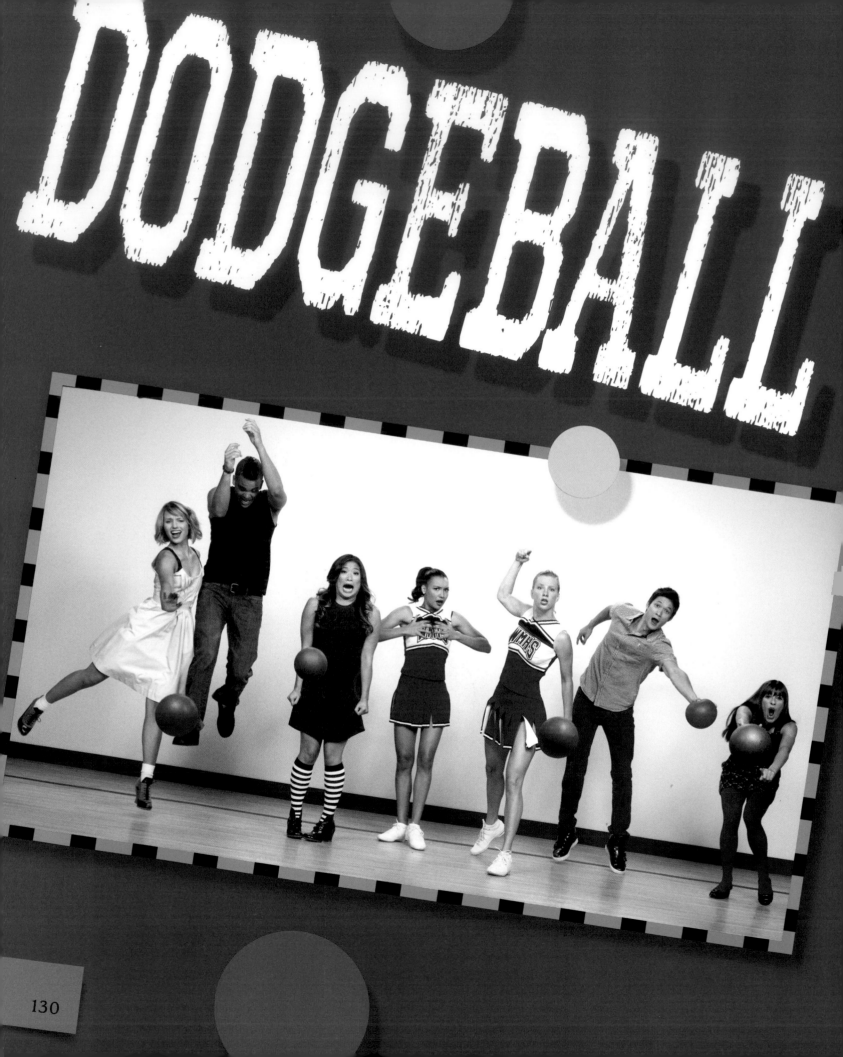

DODGEBALL

"Friends of McKinley" is sponsored, in part, by Congressman Burt Hummel.

135

Finn and Kurt,
We are so proud of both
of you!
Love,
Mom and Dad

To our dearest shining star, Rachel,
You have worked hard for this moment.
We are always proud of you.
Love,
Dad and Dad

McKinley High seniors,
Congratulations from the dads of the shining star!

Leroy Berry and Hiram Berry (Rachel's dads)

Blaine and Kurt—You'll always be Warblers to us!

THE WARBLERS, DALTON SCHOOL

WOHN News, *there when McKinley High graduates make the news...for good or bad.*

Congratulations, Class of 2012.
Get your engines started...
It's time to speed into the future!

Hummel TIRES & LUBE

Sugar,

You're the sweetest and best around!

Love,
Daddy
Al Motta—
Motta Pianos

Best wishes, seniors!
We'll be here for you when
your little princess
is ready to compete.

I smell a duet
coming on…
Congrats, seniors!
—*April Rhodes*

Seniors,
Let's go get
some tacos!

—Holly Holiday

Autographs

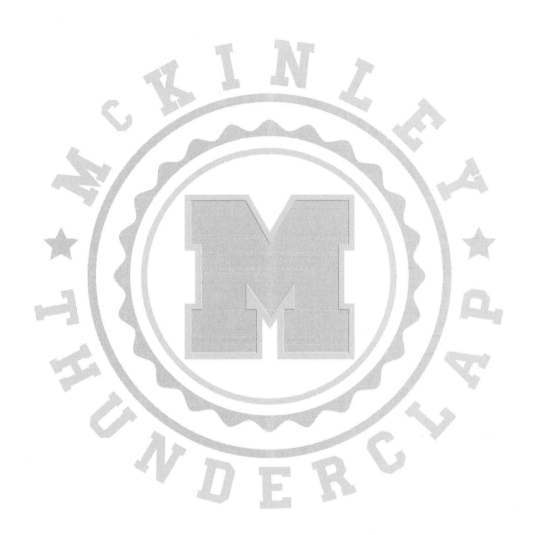

Autographs

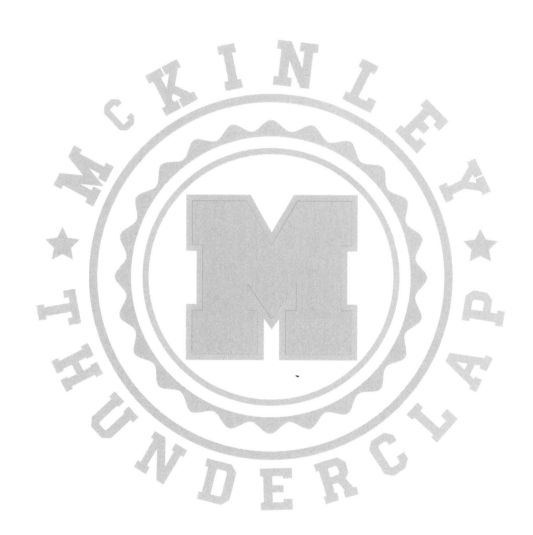

Autographs

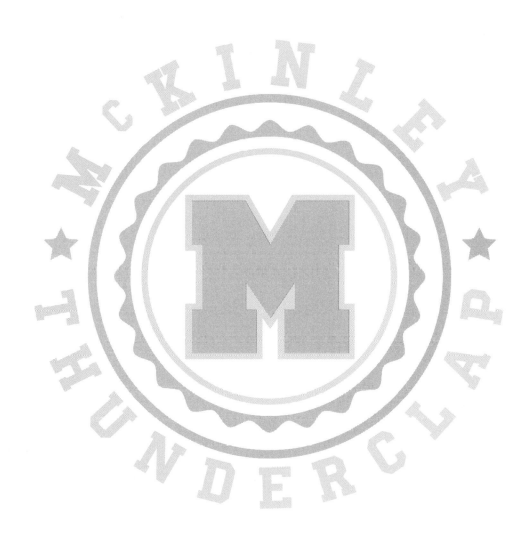

Autographs

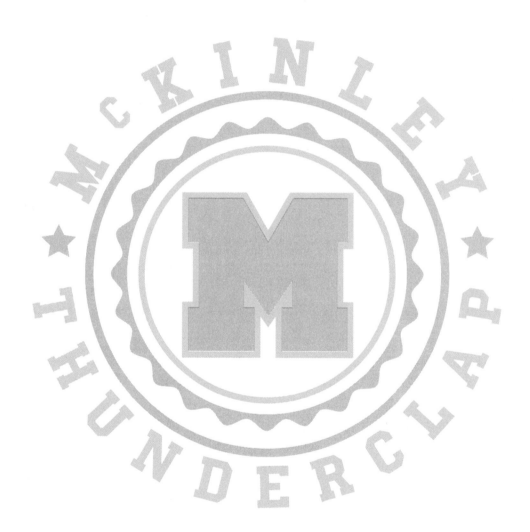